THE SPIRIT OF
ENGLAND

Sheep grazing on Chagford Common on an early autumn morning.

THE SPIRIT OF ENGLAND

SIMON McBRIDE

Foreword by Winston Graham

Webb & Bower

MICHAEL JOSEPH

DEDICATION
To Sarah, Polly, Josh and Charlie

ACKNOWLEDGEMENTS
*I would like to thank Peter Wrigley for designing the book
with such care and commitment; also my thanks to Alyson Gregory
for her endless enthusiasm and gentle approach to the editing.
I would like to thank Webb & Bower for giving me so many
lovely books to do over the past seven years and especially to
Delian Bower, a good friend. My thanks to all those farmers
whose land I've crossed – I hope you didn't mind.
I would also like to thank my parents for their help and concern
through the years and especially to my father for opening his
darkroom door. Finally, I would like to thank my wife, Sarah,
and my children Polly, Joshua and Charlie for their continual
support and encouragement despite my many long absences.*

First published in Great Britain 1989 by
Webb & Bower (Publishers) Limited
9 Colleton Crescent, Exeter, Devon EX2 4BY
in association with Michael Joseph Limited
27 Wright's Lane, London W8 5TZ

Penguin Books Ltd, Registered Offices: Harmondsworth, Middlesex
England
Viking Penguin Inc, 40 West Street, New York, New York 10010, USA
Penguin Books Australia Ltd, Ringwood, Victoria, Australia
Penguin Books Canada Ltd, 2801 John Street, Markham, Ontario,
Canada L3R 1D4
Penguin Books (NZ) Ltd, 182–190 Wairau Road, Auckland 10, New Zealand

Designed by Peter Wrigley

Production by Nick Facer/Rob Kendrew

Text and illustrations Copyright © 1989 Simon McBride

British Library Cataloguing in Publication Data

McBride, Simon.
The Spirit of England.
1. England. Landscape.
I. Title.
719'.0942

ISBN 0–86350–288–1

Library of Congress 88–83975

Typeset in Great Britain by P&M Typesetting Limited, Exeter, Devon
Colour reproduction by Peninsular Repro Service Limited, Exeter, Devon
Printed and bound in Great Britain by Purnell Book Production Limited, Paulton, Bristol.

CONTENTS

Near Barnstaple, north Devon.

The spring tide at Treyarnon, Cornwall.

FOREWORD

Earth's crammed with heaven
And every common bush afire with God;
But only he who sees, takes off his shoes,
The rest sit round it and pluck blackberries.

Thus said Elizabeth Barrett Browning, who knew a thing or two.

It is the responsibility and the pleasure – or should be – of every poet, artist, photographer, writer to see 'the burning bush', as it were, and to convey to his readers, gazers, critics, admirers, something of the world of nature or human nature, which he personally discerns and can offer specially to them. After he has spoken, or depicted it, as best he can, there are, one hopes, more people taking off their shoes and fewer just plucking the blackberries.

In observing the work of a fine photographer like Simon McBride one learns to see things through his eyes and not one's one. Often they are the familiar things which are so well known as to be taken for granted: fields, trees, mountains, fells, lakes, waterfalls. He observes them afresh; and in discovering a new sight one discovers a new beauty.

I first met him in 1981, when the book *Poldark's Cornwall* was projected, and it was suggested that as I provided the text he should provide the illustrations to the text. At this time I knew nothing of his background. Now I know that he comes of Lancashire, Irish and Cornish stock, that he left England with his parents when a year old and lived in Kenya until he was thirteen, when he came back to England to school. By then the African scene was firmly implanted and he has since returned many times. While training as a graphic designer in England he came to the conviction that photography was to be his main preoccupation in life, and when a friend sent him an air ticket to return to Africa – to Rhodesia, as it then was – it offered him the opportunity to develop his twin interests together; and he stayed there for three years as a press photographer. Back in England he took a degree in African Studies at London University, then he returned to Africa once more, covering the wars in Zimbabwe, Angola, Mozambique – and the riots in Soweto.

In 1980 he married, and by the time I met him he was settled in the West Country as an independent and freelance photographer.

After a preliminary meeting in London to discuss the book I saw him next in Cornwall in the summer of 1982. My wife and I were on holiday and the weather had been frightful; but one day, which had dawned burdened with the direst, most ominous forecasts of the weather men, had turned contrarily first into fitful and then blazing sunshine, with a rising sea, air like cool wine; bliss. Simon discovered us in our secret cove, the only couple visible, in bathing costumes, soaking up the sun. He wobbled down the precipitous path burdened with cameras, and at first was put out by a rash of caravans disfiguring the distant view. We all sat talking until the long day was near its end, and so climbed the path; then he and I strolled across the cliffs and down to the next unspoiled cove, where he took many more pictures of sea and sun and cliff and me and corrugated sand.

The following day, when the weather had returned to type, we toured round Cornwall, also the day after that, when his indefatigable energy and determination never to be satisfied with second best were much in evidence. During that summer and autumn he must have often returned to Cornwall, but then alone, seeking out the places I had mentioned in the book but seeking to create his own synthesis.

Recently a cynic said that a few generations ago England had been a country of beauty, now it was becoming a country of beauty spots. This book, *The Spirit of England*, I think disproves it. All the pictures are modern – taken, that is, within the last six years – and they show the extraordinary diversity of scene and mood and interest that such a small island can contain; and illustrate that so much is as yet unspoiled and some at least, thank God, unspoilable.

Simon is a loner, and there is a marked absence of human beings in the photographs in this book. He likes to work alone and have long periods to himself, particularly when hunting the scene he is going to shoot. He talks to himself and the sky and the countryside, persuading them to arrange themselves to suit his mood. Design is in all of them, as in all good paintings, an arrangement that comes into being and settles into perpetuity when the camera at last clicks. In some of these pictures there is a sense of foreboding, as if a brooding scene had sparked off his own dark mood and fused with it.

But the drama of lowering skies, of mountainous waves, of lonely moors, of spouting fountains merging with stormy sun-shot clouds, can give way to the tranquillity of streams and shimmering lakes and the homeliness of thatched cottages and the fishing boat's return. For Simon is no misanthrope and can enjoy as well as anyone the company of his fellow men. And when he chooses humanity for his subject, whether it is a black baby rolling in the straw in Zimbabwe or a Cornish miner dirty and cheerful after a day's chore, he brings the same talent to bear on it, the artistic eye which goes so far beyond mere expertness.

Look at these pictures and study and enjoy them all, for it is a remarkable collection which should establish Simon McBride as one of the foremost photographers of today.

It's really all in what Mrs Browning said, and she said it again in another poem, even more explicitly.

The poet hath the child's sight in his breast
And sees all new: what oftenest he has viewed
He views with the first glory.

WINSTON GRAHAM

8

INTRODUCTION

My first vivid recollection of photography was when I entered my father's darkroom, a wooden hut at the end of our sprawling garden in Africa. I was five years old and can still remember the sheer magic of entering this orange-lit world of pungent, acidic smells where images appeared mysteriously on bits of white paper floating in trays of yellow liquid. I still like to think of it in these basic, mystical forms. I have never been interested in understanding all the chemical elements and optical equations that seem to control the mechanics of that strange half-lit world.

To add to the mystery of my father's darkroom, the electricity was provided by a generator which ran the sawmills up the road. Whenever a large log hit the saw, the dimly lit room would become even darker, and the enlarger would struggle to get the image on to the paper; my father would sigh and count another 'one-thousand-and-twenties'. Then we would peer into the yellow dish straining for a first glimpse that would show Laddie, our dog, posing in the driveway. Oh! The magic of it. I still get that same thrill today when I'm printing, which alas isn't often enough.

I worked in black and white photography for the first ten years of my career, mostly in photojournalism when colour was very much 'and if you've got time, do us a roll of . . .' A few years later, magazines commissioned colour features, it was still little different from working in black and white – shoot it quickly, in sharp focus and deliver it to meet tight deadlines. There was little time to experiment with the subtlety of colour and light at the different times of the day – you had to be spot-on with your choice of exposure.

It was not until I left London, and the world of photojournalism, and moved to Devon, that I began to realize that there was more to colour than bright primaries in sharp focus so beloved of the big film manufacturers. As a photojournalist, I had worked in colour, mainly in Central and Southern Africa, covering the conflicts in Rhodesia, Mozambique, South Africa and also the Middle East crisis. The images were necessarily bright and clear, often garish, as befitted the requirements of news photography.

From the moment I saw my first print materialize in that hot and erratically lit darkroom, black and white photography monopolized my interest. I did not take a colour photograph until I was twenty-eight. Although I was at art college in the late sixties, when colour was very much part of the new, brash culture, be it clothing, pop art or psychedelic rock music, the photo gurus preached black and white, especially for landscape work. Ansel Adams, Bret Weston and the like were our idols; we followed blindly, perpetuating the belief that great photography, especially landscape work, was possible only in black and white. Ansel Adams learnt his skills before colour film had been adequately developed, both technically and commercially. By the late sixties it was there for the taking but, for the most part, we largely ignored it.

When I received my first commission from a publisher to illustrate a book, half of it in colour, it was like starting all over again. I was given a year to complete that first book, and I took every minute of it! Before meeting Winston Graham, the author of the book in question, I decided to drive down to the North Cornish coast and spend a few days absorbing the atmosphere of the place. I waited for a pleasant, bright day and took some shots of a pretty cove, and then a fishing village with boats bobbing on the water. I went home happy. The results were awful. Flat, empty chocolate-box pictures that said nothing about Cornwall.

I returned the next week on a blustery, cloud-rolling, surf-spitting day, planted my tripod at the foot of a steep cliff and pointed the lens into the spray; I remember saying to myself 'this is more like it, this is how it is'. There were some good shots among the spray-splattered, tripod-shaken images, but above all, the mood, the feel, the spirit of this beautiful coastline, slowly began to emerge.

At this time I became ever more aware of the diverse chemistry of this small part of England. It was not just the sun and sea and beaches that I had always imagined. Because Cornwall is a peninsula facing the south-westerly airstreams and ocean currents, it suffers from more types of 'weather' than many parts of the British Isles. In one day I have experienced a misty dawn, a hail storm, a flurry of snowflakes, bright sunshine, torrential rain, finally finishing off with a glorious sunset – all in all a photographer's dream! However, I have also sat through four days of dense sea-fog wondering whether I would ever see the granite church perched in the far corner of the churchyard just a few yards away. But I have learnt that patience is an essential virtue for all those aspiring to be landscape photographers. When the mists started rolling away at the end of the fourth day I got my picture. It said everything about that little church standing alone on the edge of Bodmin Moor.

I have become addicted to the vagaries of the English climate. There are so many interminable frustrations and so many unexpected rewards. The light is never the same on any two consecutive days. Even the mists and the fog proffer subtle changes: a grey-blue light one day, a creamy-yellow the next.

A fellow photographer, who lived and worked in California, once offered me his sympathy after a visit to England. He claimed to be able to photograph outdoors for seven days a week, fifty-two weeks of the year, in the most glorious weather. 'You might as well work in a studio', was my reply. I like the challenge of our unpredictable climate despite those endless, grey, drizzly days that seem to envelope us at various unspecified times through the year.

Extensive travel has taught me that no place ever looks the same when you return. So what does a place *really* look like? Does it depend on the time of day you saw it? Or on the season of the year? Or even the direction from which you approached it? I think, above all, the light conditions leave an indelible imprint on the mind. People often talk of the 'dramatic sky', or a 'misty haze' when describing a scene that has caught their eye. I have photographed a lake throughout a whole day. The way light and shadow, wind and rain altered not only the mood, but also the shape and form of the lake and its surroundings, was quite astonishing.

I would never suggest that the land itself, in whatever form it appears, is unimportant; the geomorphology of an area does influence prevailing weather patterns. But I do not think that landscapes have to be well defined in terms of large mountains, or sweeping vistas or raging rivers. Fortunately in England, because nothing is on the really grand scale, there is an abundance of ever-changing landscapes. In Africa, I have driven for three days across the same plain without a discernible change in scenery or light. In England I have walked for a day across Exmoor encountering undulating, heather-clad hills, steep-

sided, treeless valleys, high, ditched boundary lanes and wooded river valleys crossed by ancient granite bridges.

Natural resources have endowed successive generations with the materials to stamp a personality on certain regions. Hence, we have the Cotswolds, a geographically defined region of hills intersected by small meandering rivers and streams, but renowned for beautiful villages of cottages built in local Cotswold stone. Likewise, the Weald, the Chilterns, the Lakes, the Fens and the Dales are uniquely distinctive regions within the glorious patchwork of natural beauty that we call England.

This great variety of landscape presents endless opportunities for the photographer. Ever since that blustery morning at the foot of the cliff in Cornwall, I have enjoyed the challenge of the elements. If I have felt cold and windswept, then I am sure the tree standing alone on the moor felt the same way. A photographer must feel a sense of intimacy with his subjects. I have stood alone at dawn and shared the pleasure of the warming shafts of sun with the wet grasses and the tightened leaves. You have to be there. As Capa, the great war photographer, always said, 'You have to get closer, get closer'.

I am always alone when taking my photographs but never lonely. I often talk to my surroundings and have had the odd quizzical look from a passing hiker. On occasion, I have lost my temper with the hiker who eats his sandwiches in the centre of my shot, but then I suppose I was spoiling his view as well.

One of the joys of being a photographer is to walk, and walk, and walk. Unfortunately, one consequence of hiking all over the British Isles with camera equipment in tow, is the onset of chronic back trouble. I have never been an equipment freak and have always kept it to a minimum; now it's down to bare essentials. In a way that is a good thing, because I now think and look even harder. I am continually surprised by how little we look at our landscape. We have all seen it either at first hand or through media imagery but we don't really *look* at it.

This book does not pretend to be a definitive view of England. It is, rather, a personal selection of images that attempts to capture the diversity and spirit of this country that I love. I hope that those who want to look, appreciate and understand this land, might be tempted by these photographs to rise a little earlier and stay a little later.

SIMON MCBRIDE

THE SPIRIT OF
ENGLAND

A secret sandy cove, typical of many of the delights of the north Cornish coast.

The incoming tide on a late summer's evening. Russey Beach, Cornwall.

Dozmary Pool, on Bodmin Moor, Cornwall. Here Sir Belvedere is reputed to have flung King Arthur's sword, to be caught by an arm rising out of the water.

The 'Marquess' anchored off St Michael's Mount, Cornwall.
Shortly afterwards it sank in a storm off Bermuda.

The church of St Bartholomew, Warleggan, Bodmin Moor, Cornwall.

The thirteenth-century church of St-Just-in-Roseland, Cornwall.

Boconnoc, Bodmin Moor, Cornwall.

A 'Jack and Jane' wall – a traditional Cornish construction.

The Tamar Bridge, gateway to Cornwall, emerging through early morning mists.

The harbour at Polperro in Cornwall.

The viaduct over the River Tamar, Calstock, Cornwall.

The Dartmoor village of Widecombe in winter.

Cattle grazing at dusk below Hay Tor, Dartmoor.

The Norman church of St Michael, on wind-swept Brentor, Dartmoor.

The Longstone at Merrivale, Dartmoor.

A marshy pool on Okehampton Common.

A farmer harvests a 'new take' near Fernworthy Forest on Dartmoor.

Dartmoor ponies drinking at the pool below Sharpitor, Dartmoor.

Buckland-in-the-Moor, Dartmoor.

Slapton Ley: a fresh-water lake separated from the sea by a bank of shingle. American forces practised their D-day landings here in 1944. It is now a nature reserve.

Fishermen pulling in their nets at sunset on the Exe Estuary.

Exeter Cathedral at dawn.

Bickleigh on the River Exe, Devon.

Inquisitive heifers at the field gate in mid-Devon.

Dawn mists envelope the mid-Devon countryside.

The distinctive red cliffs of east Devon at Budleigh Salterton, looking towards Littleham Cove.

Rams Horn Pond, Braunton, north Devon in mid-winter.

New Bridge on the River Taw, near Barnstaple, north Devon.

Icy waterfall, above Watersmeet, Exmoor.

Farley Water above Watersmeet, Exmoor.

Autumn on the moor: the Chains, Exmoor.

Storm on Exmoor.

Tarr Steps on the River Barle, Exmoor.

Sheep grazing at dusk, Exmoor.

*Nunney Castle, Somerset: of Norman origin, it was badly
damaged during the Civil War.*

King's Sedgemoor Drain, Somerset.

Glastonbury Tor, Somerset. According to legend here, in Avalon, King Arthur and the Holy Grail were buried.

The ruins of Glastonbury Abbey, Somerset. It was founded by St Dunstan in 940 and destroyed at the Dissolution in 1539.

Vicar's Close, Wells. A street of fourteenth-century houses.

The west front of Wells Cathedral, Somerset.

The Royal Crescent, Bath.

The Parade Gardens, Bath.

A vineyard near Bruton, in Somerset.

*Woolbridge Manor, Dorset. The bridge is sixteenth century,
the house is seventeenth century.*

Abbotsbury, the fifteenth-century Chapel of St Catherine.

Maiden Castle, Dorset, the largest iron-age fortress in Europe.

Chesil Bank, Dorset.

Weymouth Harbour, Dorset.

Sheep grazing in early morning autumnal sun, near Corfe, in Dorset.

Golden Hill, Shaftesbury, Dorset.

Greenhill Pond on Egdon Heath, Dorset.

The River Kennet, Marlborough.

Cornfield, Salisbury Plain.

Salisbury Cathedral.

Freshwater Bay, Isle of Wight.

Ventnor Pier, Isle of Wight. Unlike Shanklin Pier, it survived the storm of 1987 but was badly damaged and is now closed.

The South Downs above Cocking, Sussex.

Bodiam Castle, Sussex, built in 1386 to stop French raiders from sailing up the River Rother.

Morning mists on the South Downs above Arundel, Sussex.

Lewes, Sussex.

The lighthouse dwarfed by the cliffs of Beachy Head, Sussex.

*F*ishing *boats in the Channel, off Beachy Head.*

A windmill near Rye, Sussex.

Cornfield at dawn, Sussex.

River Cuckmere, Alfriston, Sussex. In the background is the fourteenth-century Clergy House – the first building acquired by the National Trust in 1896.

Mellow Sussex cottages, West Dean.

The Weald, Sussex.

Leeds Castle, near Maidstone, Kent in mid-winter. The lake surrounding the castle was completely frozen over when this picture was taken.

Shakespeare's cliff near Dover. The Channel Tunnel will start under these cliffs.

Greenwich, the Royal Naval College.

St James's Park, London, looking towards Duck Island with Whitehall in the distance.

Little Venice, on Regent's Canal, London.

A typically elegant Georgian terraced house near Westminster.

Autumn in Green Park, London.

View of the Thames with the City in the background.

The fountains, Trafalgar Square, with the National Gallery silhouetted against the evening sky.

The Royal Deer enjoy the warmth of late-summer sun in Richmond Park.

Windsor Castle seen across the Thames in mid-winter.

An ancient track across the Berkshire Downs near Lambourn.

*The River Thames below Lechlade. Kelmscott Manor, the home
of William Morris, can be seen in the distance.*

Lower Slaughter, the Cotswolds.

*Arlington Row, former weavers' cottages at Bibury,
in the Cotswolds.*

Bourton-on-the-Water, the Cotswolds. The River Windrush flows through the centre of the village.

Bibury – the River Colne at dawn, in the late autumn.

Anne Hathaway's cottage in the hamlet of Shottery,
now part of Stratford-upon-Avon.

*H*oly Trinity Church, Stratford-upon-Avon. Shakespeare's family church and burial place.

*T*he River Avon, near Stratford-upon-Avon, Warwickshire.

Iron Bridge, Shropshire.

The River Wye near Hereford.

The River Severn below Shrewsbury, Shropshire.

The River Cam and Claire Bridge in Cambridge.

Epping Forest, Essex. The remains of the 60,000-acre hunting ground of Saxon, Norman and Tudor monarchs.

The fishing fleet on Aldeburgh Beach, Suffolk.

Morris Fen, near Peterborough, Norfolk.

Wild poppies and daisies cover a ditch at the end of a cultivated field in Suffolk.

Dusk, at Filby Broad, late summer.

The nave of Lincoln Cathedral, photographed without seating as it would have appeared in medieval times.

This power station near Gainsborough in Lincolnshire creates a powerful photographic image.

Haworth Churchyard, Yorkshire.

Haworth Moors near Haworth, Yorkshire.

Brontë Bridge, over Sladen Beck on Haworth Moor.
In the distance is Top Withens.

Top Withens, Haworth Moor, Yorkshire. The bleak ruined farmhouse is the favoured setting for Wuthering Heights.

The Packhorse Bridge, Wycoller, Lancashire.

A rookery, *Norton Conyers, Yorkshire, at dusk.*

117

The medieval city gate, York.

Honister Pass at dusk, the Lake District, Cumbria.

A walled lane, Rydal, the Lake District, Cumbria.

Rydal Water at daybreak in late summer, Cumbria.

*Aira Force waterfalls flowing down into Ullswater,
Cumbria.*

Grasmere – a tranquil part of the Lake District loved by William and Dorothy Wordsworth.

The Cheviot Hills near Wooller, Northumberland.

Bamburgh Castle, Northumberland.

Hadrian's Wall, Northumberland.

Thirwall Common, Northumberland.

NOTES

I am not obsessed with equipment. I strongly believe you should use the camera that feels right in your hands.

For landscape photography I have always felt happiest using 35mm SLR cameras. They are easy to use, are not very heavy, and above all, offer what I feel to be the most natural format for landscapes. 35mm cameras and lenses have been at the forefront of technological advances over the last ten years and many of the lenses now match those used in large-format photography.

The lens is the most important item in any photographer's equipment bag. If you put a cheap lens on a very expensive, sophisticated camera body, the results will be inferior to those you would have obtained using a good lens on a cheap body. The shutter is the most important part of the camera body, and most shutters have an accuracy well within the ⅓ of a stop latitude most colour films allow. It is irrelevant whether a shutter fires at 1/250 of a second or at 1/229 of a second – there would be no discernable difference.

As a landscape photographer I have no requirement for sophisticated electronic multi-mode cameras that are extremely heavy on batteries and, at times, confusing to operate. I use Nikon F3 and FM bodies and Nikon lenses together with two good light meters, one for general incident readings, and the other for spot metering. I also use the camera TTL metering systems, and with the help of them all, I usually get acceptable exposures.

I will continually take light readings on the hand-held incident meter throughout the day, so that I am always aware of the general level of light. I invariably use a tripod, but not as a matter of course. If I am walking long distances I keep my equipment to a minimum (it makes you think a little harder), usually two cameras and four lenses and, if it's a fairly bright day, no tripod. I will always take a few rolls of fast film – just in case! However, I have often worked out the shots I want beforehand so I usually know whether a tripod will be necessary for a particular shot. Homework is very important. I have a large selection of Ordnance Survey maps which I study in detail before shooting, noting particularly where the sun rises and sets and where shadows will fall.

I think I make more telephone calls to the meteorological office than to all my friends. I also have a reliable alarm clock – this is an essential piece of equipment as I often shoot at dawn when the light is magical and there are no people around. I also like shooting at dusk when the light is doing wonderful things at the other end of the spectrum. In between, I wander around doing my homework.

I carry a variety of films to suit both the weather conditions and the times of the day. As a general rule I use three types of colour transparency film: Kodachrome 64, Kodachrome 200, and Ektachrome 800/1600. Each film has distinctive characteristics that respond to certain conditions – I have spent years searching for the right combinations. It is all rather subjective, so my choices will not be to everyone's taste.

However, I have reached the conclusion that Kodachrome 64 produces the truest colour rendition in landscape photography. It has its foibles, but they are minimal in comparison to its overall performance and ease of use. It is a film capable of producing deep saturated colours, and soft subtle tones, usually requiring very little filtration except in extreme conditions. I don't ever use 'special effect' filters, as there is no need, given the variety of light.

If I am taking photographs very early on an autumn morning, the colour temperature can be low, so to prevent a blue cold-looking tint on the film, I will use a colour correction filter to raise the temperature and produce a 'warmer' more natural-looking image. Conversely, at the end of the day I may want to 'cool' the 'over warm' effect of an orange sky. This form of technical filtration is essential when constantly taking photographs at each end of the day; it is also very useful in extreme climatic conditions, such as snow scenes or late summer evenings.

Returning to the theme of lens quality, I always use the best filters possible, as I cannot see the logic of putting a cheap piece of glass in front of a high-quality lens.

I continually experiment with different types of film in all sorts of conditions, to find the right one for the right time of day at the right time of year. It's great fun. Why not try this for yourself?

SIMON MCBRIDE